FYODOR DOSTOYEVSKY

THE GENTLE SPIRIT

A FANTASTIC STORY

TRANSLATED BY DAVID McDUFF

PENGUIN BOOKS

PENGUIN BOOKS

Published by the Penguin Group
Penguin Books Ltd, 27 Wrights Lane, London w8 5tz, England
Penguin Books USA Inc., 375 Hudson Street, New York, New York 10014, USA
Penguin Books Australia Ltd, Ringwood, Victoria, Australia
Penguin Books Canada Ltd, 10 Alcorn Avenue, Toronto, Ontario, Canada m4v 3b2
Penguin Books (NZ) Ltd, 182–190 Wairau Road, Auckland, New Zealand

Penguin Books Ltd, Registered Offices: Harmondsworth, Middlesex, England

This translation first published in Penguin Classics 1989
This edition published 1996
1 3 5 7 9 10 8 6 4 2

Translation copyright © David McDuff, 1989
All rights reserved

The moral right of the translator has been asserted

Filmset by Datix International Limited, Bungay, Suffolk
Printed in England by Clays Ltd, St Ives

From the Author

I must apologize to my readers for the fact that on this occasion the *Diary* is presented not in its usual form, but simply as a piece of narrative. It is a piece of narrative, however, which really has kept me busy for the best part of a month. At any rate, I ask my readers' forbearance.

Now about the story itself. I have headed it 'A Fantastic Story', though I must say I consider it to be a thoroughly realistic one. But in this case it is the fantastic that is real, and this is particularly true of the form of the story, something I believe it necessary to explain in advance.

The fact is that this is neither a story nor a set of diary notes. Imagine a husband whose wife, having committed suicide a few hours earlier by throwing herself out of the window, is now lying on the table. He is in a state of shock and has not yet managed to collect his thoughts. As he wanders about his room he tries to make some sense of what has happened, to 'get things into focus'. He is, what is more, a confirmed hypochondriac, one of the kind who talk to themselves. Here he is talking to himself, describing what has happened, *trying to make sense of it*. In spite of the seeming cogency of his speech, he contradicts himself several times, both in terms of logic and of emotion. He is attempting both to justify himself and to blame her, and he embarks on long explanations, displaying both insensitivity of heart and mind, and deep feeling. Little by little he really does manage to *make sense* of what has taken place and to get his thoughts 'into focus'. A number of memories that come back to him finally lead him inexorably towards *the truth*; inexorably, the truth elevates his mind and his heart. Towards the end even the tone of the narrative undergoes a change in relation to the incoherence of its beginning. The truth is revealed to the unhappy man in terms that are, at least, sufficiently clear and unambigious for him.

So much for the subject-matter. Of course, the narrative extends throughout several hours, intermittently and by starts, and is confused in form: now the huband talks to himself, now he addresses an invisible listener, some kind of judge. That is how it always is in reality. If a stenographer had been able to eavesdrop on him and write down all the words, the result might have been a little rougher, somewhat less trimmed than what I have managed to produce; but I do not believe I am wrong in claiming that the psychological sequence would probably have been the same. It is precisely this hypothesis of a stenographer who has written everything down (to await my reworking of the raw material) that I call the fantastic element in the present narrative. But something of the same sort has been permitted in art on several occasions before: for example, Victor Hugo in his masterpiece *Le dernier jour d'un condamné* used almost the same technique, and even though he did not make use of a stenographer, he permitted himself an even greater liberty, working on the assumption that a man who has been condemned to death would be able (and have the time) to make notes not only on his last day, but even in his last hour and, quite literally, at his very last moment. Yet, if the author had not permitted this fantasy, the work itself would not exist – the most realistic and truthful work of all those to have flowed from his pen.

Chapter One

WHO I WAS AND WHO SHE WAS

... You see, as long as she's still here, everything's still all right: every moment or so I go over and take a look at her; but they'll take her away tomorrow and – how will I be on my own? She's lying on a table in the day-room, they put two card-tables together, and the coffin will be here tomorrow, a white one, wrapped in white *gros de Naples*, but that's not what I wanted to say ... I spend all the time pacing about, trying to make sense of it all. I've been trying to do that for the past six hours, yet I still can't get my thoughts into focus. The trouble is, I keep pacing, pacing, pacing ... Look, this is how it happened. I shall just tell it all in order. (Order!) Ladies and gentlemen, I am far from being a literary man, as you will see; but so be it, I will tell it to the best of my understanding. That's what makes it so horrible – the fact that I understand it all!

Well, if you really want to know, that is, if I'm going to start right at the beginning – she quite simply used to

4

come to me at that time to pawn things in order to pay for an advertisement she was running in the *Voice* that said she was a governess, willing to travel out of town and give lessons in people's homes, and so on and so forth. That was at the very beginning, and I naturally didn't distinguish her from the others: she was a customer like all the rest, if you know what I mean. But after a bit I did begin to notice her. She was a thin, fair-haired little creature, of medium to average height; with me she was always slightly awkward, as if she were embarrassed about something. (I actually think she was like that with anyone she didn't know properly, and of course to her I was just the same as anyone else, in respect of my being a person, I mean, not just a pawnbroker.) As soon as she got her money she'd immediately turn tail and go scurrying off. Never said a word. The others would argue, wheedle, haggle, trying to get more; this one didn't, whatever you gave her . . . I seem to keep getting a bit confused . . . Yes; the thing that struck me first of all was the kind of stuff she brought to pawn: little silver-gilt earrings, a rubbishy little medallion – things not worth twenty copecks. She herself was quite aware they were cheap things, but I could tell by her face that to her they were treasures –

5

and they really were all that was left to her from her father and mother, I discovered that later on. Only once did I allow myself to laugh at the things she brought. That is, you see, I'd never normally dream of doing that, I try to keep a gentlemanly tone with my clients: not too many words, polite and stern. 'Sternness, sternness and sternness' – that's my motto. But she suddenly took it into her head to bring me the remnants (quite literally, I mean) of an old hareskin jacket – and I couldn't restrain myself and cracked some kind of witty remark. Dear me, how she blazed up! She had those big blue thoughtful eyes, but – what a fire had entered them! But not a word did she let fall; she simply took her 'remnants' and – left. It was at that point that, for the first time, I paid her *special* attention, and thought something of that sort about her, that is that there was something special about her. Yes – there was something else about her, I remember, that is, if you know what I mean, the main thing about her, the synthesis of it all: and that was that she was awfully young, so young that you'd have thought she was no more than fourteen. Yet at the time she was only three months short of sixteen. But that's not what I was going to say, that's not what the synthesis was. The next day she came again. I

6

discovered later on that she'd been to Dobronravov and to Mozer with that jacket, but they didn't take anything except gold, and they wouldn't even discuss it. I once took a precious stone from her (oh, a rubbishy little one) – and found myself thinking afterwards how surprising it was; I don't usually take anything except gold and silver either, yet I'd allowed her to pawn a stone. That was the second thought I had about her that time, I remember.

On that occasion, when she'd come from Mozer, that is, she brought an amber cigar-holder with her – not a bad little knick-knack, a connoisseur's item, but once again worth nothing to us, since we only handle gold. As this was only a day after her 'rebellion', I gave her a stern reception. Sternness with me takes the form of cold indifference. However, as I gave her two roubles, I couldn't help saying, with a certain degree of irritation: 'I'm only doing this *for you*; Mozer would never take an item like that.' I placed particular emphasis on the words *for you*, and said them *with a certain meaning*. I was angry. She blazed up again when she heard that *for you*, but she didn't say anything, didn't throw the money in my face, just took it – there's poverty for you! But how she blazed up! I realized I'd wounded her. And when she'd gone, I suddenly asked myself whether this victory of mine over her was worth two roubles. Ha-ha-ha! I remember I asked myself that question two times over: 'Is it worth it? Is it worth it?' And, as I laughed, I answered it to myself in the affirmative. That provided me with no end of amusement at the time. But it wasn't a bad feeling: I had a purpose, an intention; I wanted to try her out, because I'd suddenly started to have a few notions about her. That was the third way in which she began to appear *special* to me.

. . . Well, it all began from that time. Of course, I immediately started trying to find out all about her circumstances by hearsay, and I used to await her arrival with particular impatience. I had a feeling she was going to come back again soon, you see. When she arrived, I entered into polite conversation with her, displaying an uncommon degree of courtesy. I was brought up quite nicely, you see, and I do have manners. Hm. It was then that I guessed she was meek and kind. The meek and the kind don't put up much resistance, and even though they may not tell you very much about themselves, they have absolutely no idea of how to get out of a conversation: they are sparing in their replies, but they do reply, and the longer they continue the

8

more they tell you, only you must keep the pressure up, if that's what you're after. Of course, she herself told me nothing at the time. I found out about the *Voice* and all the rest later on. At the time she was advertising herself with the last of her resources, proudly at first, of course: 'Governess, willing to travel, please send conditions in sealed envelope', but then later: 'All kinds of duties accepted – teaching, lady's companion, household care, nursing, can sew', etcetera, etcetera, you know the kind of thing. Of course, all these things were added to the advertisement in several stages, and at last, when she was nearing despair, it even said: 'No salary required, board only.' But it was no good – she couldn't find a post! Then I decided to try her out one last time: I suddenly picked up that day's copy of the *Voice* and showed her an advertisement in it which read: 'Young female person, total orphan, seeks post of governess to young children, preferably in home of elderly widower. Could help with housekeeping!'

'There, you see; that was published this morning, and by this evening, as sure as fate, she'll have found a post. That's the only way to advertise!'

Again she blazed up, again her eyes lit with fire; she turned away and left at once. I was very pleased.

Actually, at the time I was sure of everything and had no worries: I knew that no one would take her cigar-holders. And by now she would even have run out of those. So it was: on the third day she came to me all pale and agitated; I gathered that something had come up at home where she lived, something pretty serious. I will explain what it was in a moment, but for now I simply want to record that I suddenly did something for her that had a bit of style, and I rose in her estimation as a result. This is what I decided to do. The thing was that she'd brought this icon (she'd summoned up the nerve to bring it) . . . Oh, listen, listen! This was when it all began, the rest of what I've been saying's just a lot of muddle . . . The fact is that now I want to remember everything, each little trivial detail, every single little touch. I want to focus my thoughts and yet – I can't, because of all the little touches, the little touches . . .

It was an icon of the Holy Mother. A Virgin and Child, done in a homely, old-fashioned style, with a gilded-silver mounting – worth – oh, about six roubles, say. I could see she was attached to it, she wanted to pawn the whole thing, without removing the mounting. I told her it would be better if she removed the mounting separately and took the icon itself home with her; for an icon's an icon, after all.

'Is there a law that forbids you to take it?'

'No, there's no law, it's just that perhaps you your-self . . .'

'All right then, remove the mounting.'

'Look, I tell you what I'll do,' I said, after a moment's thought. 'I won't remove it, but I'll put the whole thing over there in the icon-case with the other icons, under the lamp (I always keep an icon-lamp burning in my shop, right from the time I open up in the morning), and you can have ten roubles, no questions asked.'

'I don't need ten, give me five, I promise you I'll redeem it.'

'You don't want ten? Your icon's worth it,' I added, observing that her eyes had flashed again. She said nothing. I paid out five roubles to her.

'Don't be too proud, miss; I myself have been in straits like yours, and even worse, and the fact that you see me engaged in this occupation . . . Well, it's a consequence of all that I've endured . . .'

'You mean you're taking your revenge on society? Is that it?' she said, interrupting me suddenly with rather cutting mockery, which was largely innocent (general-ized, that is, because at that time she definitely didn't make any distinction between me and anyone else, so

II

she said it almost without meaning to give offence). 'Aha!' I thought. 'So that's the kind of girl you are. Now your true character's coming out. You're one of that "new movement" lot.'

'Listen,' I said, at once half jestingly and half mysteriously. 'I – am a part of that force that always wills the Evil and always does the Good . . .'

She looked at me quickly and with great inquisitiveness, in which there was a strong childish element.

'Wait . . . What sort of an idea is that? Where does it come from? I've heard it somewhere . . .'

'You needn't rack your brains; that's how Mephistopheles introduces himself to Faust. Have you read *Faust*?'

'Not . . . not very carefully.'

'Then you haven't read it at all. You must read it right through. But I see that mocking smile on your lips again. Please don't suppose I have so little taste that, in order to put a gloss on my role of pawnbroker, I'd try to get you interested in Mephistopheles. Once a pawnbroker, always a pawnbroker. I know that, miss.'

'What a strange man you are . . . Nothing could be further from my thoughts.'

What was really in her thoughts was: 'I didn't expect you to be a man of such education'; but she didn't say it. I knew, though, that that was what she was thinking. I'd made a terrific impression on her.

'Listen,' I said. 'A person can do good in any walk of life. I'm not talking about myself, of course – I take it for granted that I don't do anything except the other, but . . .'

'Of course, it's possible to do good in any kind of job,' she said, giving me a quick, penetrating look. 'In absolutely any kind of job,' she added, suddenly. Oh, I remember, I remember all those moments! And I would add too, that when these young girls, these dear young girls take it into their heads to say something clever and inspired, their faces suddenly take on such a sincere, unaffected expression, as if to say: 'Look, now I'm telling you something clever and inspired.' And it's not out of vanity, as it would be with yours truly – you really do see that she herself places an incredibly high value on it, that she believes it and considers it important and thinks that you will consider it every bit as important as she does. Oh, that sincerity! That's how they conquer us. And in her how lovely it was!

I remember – I've forgotten none of it! After she'd left my shop, I instantly made up my mind. That very same day I went off to make some up-to-date inquiries and found out everything else there was to know about her, the current details, as it were; I'd already heard all the details of her earlier life from Lukerya, their servant-woman at that time, whom I'd bribed a few days previously. Those details were so dreadful that I couldn't understand how she'd been able to laugh the way she had just then, how she could have displayed such curiosity about the words of Mephistopheles when she herself was in such a dreadful position. But – these young girls! That was what I thought about her at the time with both pride and joy, because, after all, there was a magnanimity about it, as if she were saying: 'Even though I'm on the brink of ruin, the great words of Goethe are still radiant with light.' Youth always has magnanimity, even if it's just a little, and aimed in the wrong direction. But I mean it's really her I'm talking about, and her alone. And the main thing is that at that time I already looked upon her as *my own*, and was in no doubt as to the power I had over her. That's a very voluptuous feeling, you know, when you don't have any doubts.

But what's the matter with me? If I keep on like this, how will I ever get it all into focus? Quick, quick – what I've been going on about isn't important at all. Oh, God!

A PROPOSAL OF MARRIAGE

The 'details' I found out about her can be summed up quite briefly: her father and mother had died quite a long time ago, three years earlier, and she had been left in the care of two disreputable aunts, though that is an epithet too mild to describe them. One of the aunts was a widow with a big family – six children, each younger than the other – and her sister was a nasty old maid. They were both nasty pieces of work. Her father had been a civil servant, but only in the copying department, and had had only non-hereditary gentlemanly status; it all served my purpose. I had arrived as it were from a higher world: I was, at any rate, a retired second-grade captain from a distinguished regiment, a gentleman by birth, independent, etcetera, and as for my pawnbroker's business, the aunts could only look upon that with respect. She had been living in bondage to her aunts for three years, but even so she had taken and passed an examination somewhere – she had managed to pass it, had forced herself to pass it, from under the pitiless burden of her daily toil – and this said a lot in terms of a striving for the lofty and the noble on her part! –

After all, why do you think I wanted to marry her? But I don't give a spit about me; that can wait ... As if that were what was important! She gave her aunt's children lessons, she made underwear, and eventually she ended up scrubbing floors too, and with a chest like hers. They even used quite simply to beat her, and they made her feel guilty for eating their bread. In the end, it came to the point where they planned to sell her. Ugh! I won't go into all the filthy details. Later on she told me all about it. For a whole year all this had been observed by the fat storekeeper who lived next door; he wasn't just any old storekeeper, he owned two grocery stores. He'd already salted away a couple of wives and was looking for a third when he set eyes on her: 'She's a quiet girl,' he thought. 'She's grown up in poverty, and I'll marry her for my little orphans; they could do with a mother.' He certainly had a few of those orphans. He began his suit and started negotiations with the aunts; he was fifty, too – the girl was horror-stricken. It was just about this time that she began to make such frequent visits to me, in order to pay for her advertisements in the *Voice*. At last she started to beg her aunts to let her think the matter over for just a little bit of time. This they agreed to, but only this; otherwise they merely kept on at her, saying: 'We ourselves don't know where the next bite's coming from, never mind about having an extra mouth to feed.' I already knew all about this, and that day, after what had taken place in the morning, I made my decision. That evening the grocery merchant had turned up with a fifty-copeck box of sweets from his store; she was sitting with him when I called Lukerya out of the kitchen and told her to go and whisper in her ear that I was at the front gate and that there was something I wanted to tell her without delay. I was feeling pleased with myself. In fact, all that day I'd been feeling like the cat's whiskers.

Right there at the front gate, in Lukerya's presence, I told her, dumbfounded as she was at my having asked her to come out, that for one thing I would consider it a happiness and an honour . . . and that for another she was not to wonder at my manner and at the fact that I was at her front gate: 'I'm a straightforward fellow,' I said, 'and I've gone into all the ins and outs of the matter.' And I wasn't making it up when I said I was straightforward. Oh, I don't give a spit about me. But anyway, not only did I speak with due propriety, show-ing that I was a man of good upbringing, but also with originality, and that was the main thing. Well, I mean, is there any harm in admitting it? My intention is to pass judgement on myself, and that's what I'm doing. I must present all the pros and contras, and I'm doing that, too. Afterwards I recalled the whole scene with pleasure, even though it was stupid: I bluntly declared to her, without the slightest embarrassment, that for one thing I was not particularly talented, not particularly clever, possibly not even very kind, that in fact I was rather a cheap egoist (I remember that expression, I made it up on the way there and was pleased as Punch with it) and that very, very probably I contained within me much that was unpleasant in other respects too. This was all said with a peculiar form of pride – everyone knows that manner of speaking. Of course, having nobly declared my shortcomings, I had sufficient good taste not to launch into a description of my virtues, along the lines of: 'but on the other hand, I do possess this, that and the other'. I could see that she was still terribly scared, but I didn't play anything down; indeed, observing that she was scared, I purposely laid it on thick: told her bluntly that she'd have enough food in her belly, but as for smart clothes, theatres and balls – she could forget them, except possibly later on, if I achieved my purpose. I really did get carried away by this severe line of talk. I added, also as casually as possible, that in taking up such an occupation – the running of this pawnshop, I meant – I had had only one purpose, that there was in other words a certain special circumstance . . . But I mean, I had some justification for talking like this: I really did have such a purpose and special circumstance. You see, ladies and gentlemen, I have always been the first to detest this pawnbroker's business, but actually, although it's absurd to talk to oneself in mysterious phrases, I was after all 'taking my revenge on society', I really, really, really was! The sarcastic remark she had made that morning about my 'taking my revenge' had not been justified. I mean, you see, if I'd told her in so many words: 'Yes, I'm taking my revenge on society,' she'd have burst out laughing, the way she'd done earlier, and the whole thing really would have been absurd. Yes, but by means of a subtle hint and the dropping of a mysterious phrase it seemed that it was possible to act on her imagination. In any case, I no longer had any fears: I mean, I knew that the fat storekeeper was more repugnant to her than I, and that as I stood there at her front gate I appeared as her liberator. I'd understood that, you see. Oh, a man understands the shabby things of life only too well! But was this shabby? How is a man to be judged in such circumstances? Didn't I love her even then?

But wait: I naturally made not the merest allusion to her about my doing her a good turn; oh, on the contrary: 'It's the other way round,' I wanted to say. 'It is *I* who will be indebted to *you*.' And I actually did put this into words, I couldn't resist it, and it must have sounded stupid for I noticed that fleeting smile on her face. On the whole, however, I definitely came through a winner. But wait again – if I'm really going to rake through all that filth once more, I might as well include this final piece of swinishness. I stood there, and the thought that was going through my mind was: 'I'm tall, slim, educated and – without needing to brag about it – I'm handsome.' That was what was going round in my head. And she, of course, right there at the front gate, said *yes*. But . . . but I must add this: as she stood there, it took her a long time to get through her thoughts before she uttered that *yes*. So long did she spend thinking that I was almost on the point of saying to her, 'Well?'; and actually said it: 'Well then, miss?' – making sure I got the 'miss' in.

'Wait,' she said. 'I'm thinking.'

And how serious her little face was! It bore an expression that I ought to have been able to read even then. But I was hurt. 'Can she really be choosing between me and that grocery merchant?' I thought. Oh, I understood nothing back then! Nothing, nothing at all did I understand! I remember that Lukerya came running out after me as I was leaving, stopped me en route and said hurriedly: 'God will reward you for taking our dear young lady, sir, only don't tell her that, for she's a proud one.'

A proud one, eh? I thought, I like the proud ones. The proud ones are especially attractive when . . . well, when one doesn't have any more doubts as to one's power over them! Oh, the shabby, blundering wretch that I was! Oh, how pleased with myself I felt! For I mean, as she stood there at the front gate wondering whether to say *yes* to me or not, I was amazed that there could be any such thought in her head of the type: 'If I'm to be miserable either way, mightn't it be better just to choose the very worst and have done with it – the fat storekeeper, in other words, and the sooner he beats me to death when he's drunk the better!' Eh? What do you suppose – was it something like that she was thinking?

Even now I don't know what to think, I don't know what to think about any of it. I said just now that she might have had a thought of the kind: 'I'd better choose the greater of two evils – the grocer, in other words.' But who did actually represent the greater evil at that time – I or the grocer? A grocer or a pawnbroker who could quote Goethe? There's a question for you! Some question. The answer to it is lying right there on the table, and you call it a question! Oh, I don't give a spit about myself! I'm not what matters, I don't matter at all . . . In any case, what is there left for me to do now, whether I matter or don't matter? That's what I can't for the life of me see. I'd better go to bed. I've got a headache . . .

III

THE NOBLEST OF MEN, THOUGH I MYSELF DON'T BELIEVE IT

I couldn't get to sleep. How could I have done, when there's some sort of pulse beating inside my head? I want to absorb it all into myself, all that dirt. Oh, that dirt! Oh, the dirt from which I dragged her then! I mean, she must have understood that, she must have known what I was doing! There were various thoughts that I found appealing at the time – that I was forty-one, for example, while she was only sixteen. It captivated me, that sense of inequality, it was very delightful, very delightful indeed.

For example, I planned to hold our wedding *à l'anglaise*, that's to say, just the two of us together, except perhaps for two witnesses, one of whom would be Lukerya. Then it would be straight on to the train, I thought, preferably to Moscow (actually, I had some business to attend there), where we would stay in a hotel for a couple of weeks. She opposed the idea, wouldn't allow it, and I found myself having to drive round and visit her aunts, treating them respectfully as though they were kinsfolk from whom I was taking her away. I yielded, and the aunts received their due. I even made those creatures a gift of 100 roubles each, and promised them more (not telling her about it, naturally, so as not to rub in the shabbiness of her surroundings). The aunts at once turned as meek as lambs. There was an argument, too, about the trousseau; she had almost literally nothing, but she didn't want anything, either. I managed, however, to make her concede that that would simply not do, and I provided the trousseau, for who else would have done it? Oh, I don't give a spit about myself. All the same, I did manage to get the various ideas I had through to her, so at least she knew what they were. Perhaps I was in too much of a hurry. The main thing was that right from the word go, no matter how hard she tried to restrain herself, she came rushing towards me with love, would greet me with ecstasy when I arrived in the evenings, telling me in that prattle of hers (the charming prattle of innocence!) all about her childhood, her girlhood, her parental home, her father and mother. But I immediately poured cold water on all that rapture. That was the idea. To her enthusiasm I would respond with silence – benevolent silence, of course . . . but all the same, she quickly saw that there was a difference between us and that I was a riddle. That was what I strove to be above all else – a riddle! I mean, it was possibly in order to be a riddle that I went and did this whole stupid thing! In the first place, sternness – it was to the accompaniment of a certain sternness that I took her into my household. To be brief: in spite of being so pleased with myself at the time, I created an entire system. Oh, it came pouring out without the slightest effort. And it couldn't have been any different, I had to create that system because of a certain uncompromising circumstance – but why am I doing myself down? The system was a real one. No, listen here! If you're going to judge someone, then you must judge him knowing all the facts of his case . . . Listen!

I don't know how to begin, it's really very difficult. It's when one starts trying to justify oneself – that's the hard part. Look: for example, young people despise money – I immediately put all the emphasis on money, I made it into the be-all and end-all. So much stress did I place on it that she began more and more to dry up. She'd open those big eyes of hers, listen, look at me and say nothing. Look: young people are generous, the good ones, that is, they're generous and impulsive, but they don't have much tolerance; if anything's even slightly not the way it ought to be – they show their contempt. But what I wanted was breadth of vision, I wanted to instil it into the workings of her heart, do you know what I mean? Let me take a worthless example: how would I, for example, explain my pawnbroker's business to someone with a character like that? Of course, I didn't put it as directly as that, otherwise it would have sounded as though I was asking to be forgiven for running a pawnshop; no, I made my impression by means of pride, as it were, I spoke by almost keeping silent. I'm a master at doing that, I've done it all my life and I've lived through entire tragedies on my own without saying a word. Oh, I too have been unhappy! I've been rejected by everyone, rejected and forgotten, and no one, no one knows it! And here this sixteen-year-old girl suddenly got hold of certain details about me from some shabby individuals and thought she knew everything about me, yet all the time the real me was locked up inside this breast of mine! I kept on being silent; especially, especially when she was around, right up until yesterday – but why? Because I'm a proud man. I wanted her to find out for herself, without my intervention, but not from the stories told by shabby folk – I wanted her to *guess for herself* the nature of this man, and understand him! In taking her into my household, I wanted complete respect from her. I wanted her to kneel before me in supplication for my sufferings – I deserved that. Oh, I've always been proud, I've always wanted everything or nothing! It's precisely for that reason, because I've never been one for half-measures where happiness is concerned, but have always wanted to go the whole way, that I was obliged to act like that at the time. It was as if I were saying: 'Do it for yourself – guess what I'm like and draw your own conclusions!' Because you must agree that if I myself had begun to explain and suggest things to her, beating about the bush and asking her for respect – it would have been just as if I'd been begging her for alms . . . But anyway . . . anyway, why am I telling you all this?

It's stupid, stupid, stupid, stupid! At the time I explained to her, bluntly and without mercy (I stress the fact that I did it without mercy), in so many words, that the generosity of young people was all very fine, but – it wasn't worth a brass button. Why? Because it doesn't cost them anything, because it's not something they've gained from the experience of living, it's all just 'the first impressions of existence'; no, let's see them do a bit of hard work! Generosity that doesn't cost anything is always easy, because it's just 'the boiling of the blood and an excess of energy', they're that desperate for beauty! No, try to do something that requires real greatness of spirit, something that's hard, takes a long time, doesn't make any noise, doesn't have any fine exterior, something that's done to the accompaniment of taunts and jeers, that involves much sacrifice and not a drop of glory – that involves you, illustrious man, being exposed to everyone as a villain, when really you're a better person than anyone else upon earth – go on, try to do that! But now, you'll throw in the towel! Well, I – I've spent my whole life doing nothing but trying to do something like that. At first she argued, and how, but then she began to shut up, altogether, in fact, and only her eyes opened, round and terrible as she listened, those big, big listening eyes. And . . . and, in addition to that, I suddenly saw her smile, a suspicious, quiet, nasty smile. It was with that smile on her face that I took her into my household. It's also true that she had nowhere else to go . . .

IV

PLANS AND MORE PLANS

Which one of us started it first?

Neither of us. It was something that started of its own accord right from the very beginning. I said earlier that I took her into my household to the accompaniment of a certain sternness; but right from the very beginning I toned that sternness down. Before I married her it was explained to her that she would be responsible for accepting the customers' pledges and for dispensing their cash and, I mean, she made no objection at the time (please note that). Nor was that all – she settled down to the work with positive zeal. Well, of course my apartment, the furniture in it – all that remained the same as before. There were only two rooms in my apartment: one of them was a large drawing-room, one end of which was divided off with a partition to house the pawnshop, and the other, also large, was the one which we shared and which is also the bedroom. My furniture is poor stuff; even her aunts' stuff was better. I keep my icon-case and lamp in the room with the pawnshop; the other room contains my bookcase with a few books, and my safe, of which I keep the keys; well, and there's a bed, and some tables and chairs. Before I married her I told her that for our upkeep – that's to say, for the food to be consumed by her, Lukerya and myself – one rouble was to suffice, and that was all: 'I must have 30,000 roubles in three years' time,' I told her, 'and if we spend any more then I won't be able to save enough.' She made no difficulties, but even so I raised the sum for our allowance, without being asked, by thirty copecks. The same went for the theatre. Before we married, I had told her that we would not go to the theatre, yet now I proposed to visit it once a month, and to sit in a decent part of the house, in the stalls. We went together three times; we saw *The Pursuit of Happiness* and *Songbirds*, I believe. (Oh, I don't give a spit, I don't give a spit!) In silence we would go, and in silence we would return. Why, why from the very beginning did we adopt that habit of being so silent together? I mean, to start with we didn't have any quarrels – there was just that silence. I remember that at that time she used to keep giving me looks in secret; when I noticed this I became even more silent. It's true that it was really I who insisted on the silence, not her. Once or twice there were outbursts of passionate emotion on her part, and she would rush to embrace me; but since these outbursts were morbid, hysterical ones, and what I wanted from her was assured happiness, mingled with respect, I received them coldly. And I was right to; for on each occasion she had one of those outbursts we quarrelled the following day.

Well, we didn't have any quarrels, but there was the silence and – and an increasingly cheeky look on her face. 'Rebellion and independence' – that was what was going on, only she was no good at it. Yes, that meek face of hers was getting cheekier and cheekier. Would you believe it – she was beginning to find me repulsive. At any rate, that was what I'd come to assume. And that at times she lost her temper and had those outbursts, of that there was no doubt. She'd actually make sniffy remarks about our poverty, a fine thing coming from something who'd only just emerged from all that filth and destitution and scrubbing of floors! You see, ladies and gentlemen, it wasn't really poverty, it was economy, and there was a fair abundance of the essentials: linen, for example, and facilities for personal cleanliness. It always used to be one of my fantasies that cleanliness in a man is something a woman finds attractive. Actually, it wasn't our poverty that got up her nose so much as what she called my stinginess in our household budget. It was as if she were saying: 'Oh, so he thinks he's being single-minded, showing me what a firm character he has.' She suddenly started saying she didn't want to go to the theatre any more. And her mocking smile got worse and worse . . . And I made my silence more intense, more and more intense.

Shouldn't I have tried to justify myself? After all, the pawnshop was the most important thing. Listen: I knew that a woman, particularly one only sixteen years old, cannot avoid being in complete subordination to a man.

Women don't have any originality; that — that's an axiom, one which I find valid even now! What's that lying on the table out there? The truth's the truth, and not even Mill himself can make it otherwise! But a woman who loves, oh, a woman who loves idolizes even the vices, the evil-doings of her beloved. He himself would be incapable of seeking out the kind of justifications she will discover for such villainies. That shows generosity of spirit, but it is not original. It is solely her lack of originality that has been woman's undoing. I say it again: why do you point at the table? Is there really anything original about what's lying on that table? Oh, no.

Listen: at the time I was certain that she loved me. I mean, she'd throw herself at me and kiss my neck, too. When I say she loved me, it might be more correct to say that she wanted to love me. Yes, that's what it was: she wanted to love me, she sought to love me. But the thing was that in my case there weren't any villainies for her to seek justifications for. You may say I'm a pawnbroker — that's what everyone says. So what if I am? After all, there must be reasons why I, the most magnanimous of men, should have become a pawnbroker. You see, ladies and gentlemen, there are certain ideas . . . I mean, there are some ideas which if you say them out loud, put them into words, sound awfully stupid. You feel ashamed of them. Why? Oh, for no reason. Because we're all rubbish and can't bear the truth, if I'm not mistaken. Just now I called myself 'the most magnanimous of men'. It sounds ridiculous, yet I mean it: it really was the case. I mean, it really is true, it's God's own truth! Yes, at the time I *had a right* to want to look after my own interests by opening this pawnshop. What was in my mind was something like this: 'You've rejected me (people, that is), you've banished me with contemptuous silence. You have answered my passionate striving towards you with an insult that will last for the rest of my life. So now I am within my rights if I protect myself from you with a wall, gather together these 30,000 roubles and finish my life somewhere on the southern shores of the Crimea amidst mountains and vineyards, on an estate of my own, bought with that 30,000, and, most important of all, far away from all of you, but with no rancour towards you, with the ideal in my soul, with the woman beloved of my heart, with my family, if God sends me one, and – helping the local inhabitants.' Well, of course, it's right for me to say this about myself now, but what could have been more stupid than for me to have told her all that out loud, in all its extravagant detail? That was why I maintained that proud silence, that was why we sat there saying nothing. For how much of it could she possibly have understood? She was only sixteen, in her first youth – what could she have made of my self-justifications, my sufferings? Here there were straight-forwardness, ignorance of life, the easily won convictions of youth, the nocturnal blindness of those 'Schöne Seelen', yet what really mattered was the pawnshop and – basta! (And wasn't I a villain in my pawnshop, didn't she see how I behaved, watching to see if I charged too much?) Oh, how terrible is earth's truth! That meek, lovely creature, that heaven – she was a tyrant, the insupportable torturer and tyrant of my spirit! I mean, I would be doing myself an injustice were I not to say that! Do you think I didn't love her? Who can say I didn't love her? Look: there was an irony here, a cruel irony of fate and nature! We are cursed, people's lives are in general cursed! (Mine particularly!) I mean, I realize now that somewhere along the line I went wrong. Something didn't turn out the way it was supposed to. Everything was clear, my plan was clear as the heavens: 'I'll be proud, stern, requiring no inner consolation, but suffering in silence.' So indeed it was, I wasn't lying, I wasn't lying! 'Later on she'll see for herself that it involved greatness of soul, only she hadn't been able to perceive it – and when she begins to surmise that, I'll go up in her esteem tenfold, and she'll fall to the ground before me, clasping her hands in supplication.' That was my plan. But then I forgot something, or left something out. There was something I was unable to do. But enough of this, enough. And who is there to ask for forgiveness now? What's done is done. Have more courage, man, and be proud! It's not you who are to blame! . . .

V

THE MEEK GIRL REBELS

The quarrels began when she suddenly took it into her head to start paying out money on her own initiative, assessing articles the customers brought in above their true value, and even on a couple of occasions doing me the honour of engaging me in dispute on this subject. I did not accept the challenge. But then the captain's widow turned up.

35

This old captain's widow had come to me with a medallion – it had been a gift from her husband when he had been alive, you know the sort of thing, a keepsake. I'd let her have thirty roubles for it. She'd begun to whimper piteously, begging me to look after the thing – of course I always do that anyway. Well, to be brief, she suddenly came back five days later in order to exchange it for a bracelet that wasn't worth eight roubles; naturally I refused. I think she must have guessed something from the look in my wife's eyes, but anyway she came again when I wasn't there, and my wife let her substitute it for the medallion.

Learning of it that same day, I began to speak quietly, but firmly and in a reasoned manner. She was sitting on the bed, looking at the floor and scuffing the toe of her right foot on the carpet (one of her favourite gestures); there was a nasty smile on her lips. Then, without raising my voice at all, I told her calmly that the money was *mine*, that I had a right to take my *own* view of life and that when I invited her to come into my house I had, after all, not concealed anything from her.

She suddenly leapt up, quivering all over and – would you believe it – began to stamp her feet at me; she was a wild beast, it was a fit, it was a wild beast having a fit. I froze with amazement; never had I anticipated such extraordinary behaviour. But I did not lose my presence of mind, I did not even move at all, and again in my previous quiet voice I told her that I would not be asking her to help me in my work any more. She laughed in my face and walked out of the apartment.

The point was that she had no right to walk out of the apartment. She went nowhere without me – that had been our understanding even before she had married me. Towards evening she returned; I said not a word.

First thing the next morning she again left the apartment, and she did the same the day after that as well. I closed up the shop and set off to her aunts' place. After the wedding I had broken off relations with them – I didn't invite them and they didn't invite me. Now it turned out that she hadn't been to see them either. They listened to my tale with curiosity and laughed in my face: 'Just what you deserve,' they said. But I had expected their laughter. Then I offered the younger aunt, the unmarried one, an inducement of 100 roubles, giving her twenty-five in advance. Two days later she came to me: 'There's an officer mixed up in it,' she said. 'His name's Yefimovich, he's a lieutenant who used to be a chum of yours in your old regiment.' I was thoroughly amazed. This Yefimovich had done me more harm than anyone else in the regiment, and a month previously, being a shameless sort of fellow, had looked in at my shop a couple of times, pretending he wanted to pawn various items, though I remembered that he and my wife had then begun to laugh at me. At the time I'd gone up to him and told him not to dare to come and call on me like this, bearing in mind the way matters stood between us; but as for there being anything between them, I had no ideas of anything of that sort at all – I just thought he was an insolent lout. But this aunt suddenly told me that an appointment had been arranged for him to see her, and that the whole business was being managed by a woman named Yulia Samsonovna who was an old friend of the aunts, a widow and a colonel's wife, too – 'She's the person your wife visits now,' she said.

I will abridge this part of the action. Altogether, this business had cost me nearly 300 roubles, but within two days it had been arranged that I should stand in the next room behind closed doors and eavesdrop on the first rendezvous Yefimovich and my wife had alone together. On the eve of this event, as I waited for it to happen, there took place between her and myself a scene which, though brief, was to be of very great significance for me.

She returned as evening was drawing in, sat down on the bed, gave me a mocking look and started to scuff her foot on the carpet. Suddenly as I watched her the thought flashed into my head that all this last month or, rather, for the two weeks before this, she had not been behaving in character; that she had even, one might have said, been behaving like someone of opposite character: a wilful, aggressive creature was making its appearance – I cannot say shameless, but disorderly and in active search of trouble. Asking for it. Her meekness was, however, getting in the way. When a female like that starts to grow wilful, even when she oversteps the limit, it is still evident that she is pushing herself to do it, driving herself on, and that it is impossible for her to cope with her own sense of chastity and shame. That's why females of that type sometimes kick over the traces in such an immoderate manner that one finds it hard to believe one's own observing intellect. The ones who are accustomed to depravity, on the other hand, always try to play the whole thing down; they do the most loathsome things, but under a pretence of order and propriety, things in which they claim to be your superior.

'Is it true that you were dumped out of the regiment because you were scared to fight a duel?' she asked suddenly, out of the blue, and her eyes began to flash.

'Yes, it's true; the verdict of my fellow-officers was that I be asked to leave the regiment, though as a matter of fact I'd already sent in my papers.'

'They expelled you as a coward?'

'Yes, cowardice was what I was found guilty of. But the reason for my refusing to fight that duel was not that I was a coward, but that I didn't want to submit to their tyrannical verdict and challenge a man to a duel when I didn't feel I'd been insulted. You know,' I said, unable to restrain myself, 'the act of rebelling against that kind of tyranny and accepting all the consequences that followed took a lot more courage than any duel.'

I really couldn't hold myself in check, and with this sentence I found myself launching into a bout of self-justification; that was just what she had been waiting for – for me to humiliate myself again. She burst into malicious laughter.

'And is it true that for the next three years you wandered around the streets of St Petersburg like a tramp, begging for coppers and spending the nights in billiard saloons?'

'I even spent nights down at the Haymarket, in the Vyazemsky. Yes, it's true; in the life I led after leaving the regiment there was a lot of shame and degradation, though not degradation of a moral kind, because even then I myself hated what I was doing. It was merely a degradation of my mind and my will, and was provoked exclusively by despair at my situation. However, it passed . . .'

'Oh, but now you're a somebody — a financier!' she said.

This was a reference to the pawnshop. But by this time I'd managed to get a hold on myself. I could see that she was eager for explanations that would be humilating for me — but I didn't give her any. Just then a customer rang the doorbell, and I went out to the main room to attend to him. Afterwards, an hour later, when she had suddenly put her things on in order to go out, she stopped in front of me and said:

'You didn't tell me anything about that before we got married, did you?'

I made no reply and she went on her way.

Well, so the following day I stood behind the door of that room and listened to my fate being decided; I had a revolver in my pocket. She was sitting at the table, all dressed up, and Yefimovich was giving himself airs in front of her. And what do you know? It all turned out (I think this speaks in my favour), it all turned out exactly as I had anticipated and supposed it would, even though I wasn't aware of having done so. I don't know whether I'm making myself clear or not.

This is how it turned out. I listened for a whole hour, and for a whole hour I witnessed a duel between a woman of the most noble sublimity and a worldly, depraved, slow-witted reprobate with the soul of a reptile. Where, I thought in a state of shock, had this simple, this reticent creature learnt all this? The wittiest author of high-society farces could not have created this scene of mockery, loud, simple laughter and the sacred contempt felt by virtue for vice. What brilliance there was in the things she said, in the little *bons mots* she uttered; what sharpness of wit there was in her quick answers, what truth in the censure she apportioned! And, at the same time, what simplicity, almost maidenly in character. She laughed in his face at his declarations of love, at his gestures, his proposals. Having arrived at the heart of the matter in one fell swoop, and not expecting to encounter resistance, he fairly came down a peg or two. At first I might have been forgiven for thinking that all this was just coquetry on her part – 'the coquetry of a being depraved but witty, adopted with the aim of showing herself off to best advantage'. But no, the truth had begun to shine like the sun and doubt was out of the question. Being inexperienced in such matters, she had only been able to arrange this rendezvous out of an unnatural and impetuous hatred for me, but when it had come to the crunch – her eyes were opened at once. The creature had been simply in a tearing rush to insult me by any means possible but, having decided on the present piece of filth, had been unable to endure the mess. And could she, sinless and pure as she was, possessed of an ideal, have been seduced by Yefimovich or any of those other high-society reprobates? On the contrary; he merely aroused her laughter. The truth ascended from her soul in its entirety, and indignation called forth sarcasm from her heart. I repeat: towards the end this buffoon fell into a complete daze and sat frowning, scarcely able to reply, so that I even began to get worried lest he risk insulting her out of base revenge. And I will say it again: I think it speaks in my favour that I overheard this scene practically without any amazement whatsoever. It was as if I had encountered something familiar. It was as if I had gone there in order to encounter it. I had gone without believing there could be any accusation against her, even though I'd taken my revolver along in my pocket – that's the truth! And could I really have imagined her to be any different? Why did I love her, why did I value her so highly, why had I married her? Oh, of course, at the time I was only too convinced that she hated me, but I was also convinced that she was chaste and pure. I brought the scene to an end suddenly, by opening the door. Yefimovich leapt up, and I took her by the arm and requested her to come outside with me. Yefimovich recovered himself and suddenly burst into resonant peals of laughter:

'Oh, far be it from me to interfere with the sacred rights of conjugality! Take her with you, by all means take her with you! But I tell you what,' he shouted after me, 'though no man of honesty would ever fight you, out of respect for your lady wife I declare myself at your service . . . That is, if you're prepared to take the risk . . .'

'Did you hear that?' I said, making her stop for a second on the threshold.

After that, not a word passed between us all the way home. I led her by the arm, and she offered no resistance.

On the contrary, she was in a terrible state of shock, but this lasted only until we reached the apartment. On our arrival there she sat down on a chair and fixed me with a stare. She was extremely pale; though her lips had immediately creased themselves into a mocking smile, she was looking at me with a stern, solemn challenging expression, and appeared for those first few moments to be seriously convinced that I was going to kill her with my revolver. But I took the revolver out of my pocket in silence and put it on the table. She looked at me, and then at the revolver. (Please note: this revolver was familiar to her. I had acquired it and kept it loaded from the very first day I had opened my shop. When starting my business I had decided not to keep either enormous dogs or a strong manservant, like Mozer does, for example. My cook lets my visitors in. But those who engage in our trade cannot be without some means of self-defence in case of trouble, and I had bought a loaded revolver. In the early days when she had only just entered my household, she had been very interested in that revolver, had asked me questions about it, and I had even explained to her its mechanism and mode of operation and had, moreover, persuaded her to do some target practice with it. Please note all

45

this.) Paying no attention to her frightened stare, I lay down on the bed, half-undressed. I was very tired; it was by then nearly eleven o'clock. She continued to sit in the same place, not moving a limb, for another hour or so; then she snuffed out the candle and lay down, still with her clothes on, she too, on the sofa over by the wall. It was the first time she had not slept with me – please note that, too.

VI

A TERRIBLE REMINISCENCE

Now that terrible reminiscence . . .

I woke up the next morning, at about eight I think it was, for the room was almost completely light. I woke up at once, fully conscious, and opened my eyes suddenly. She was standing by the table and was holding my revolver. She had not seen me wake up and was unaware that I was looking at her. And suddenly I saw that she had begun to approach me with the revolver in her hands. Quickly, I closed my eyes and pretended to be fast asleep.

She reached the bed and stood over me. I could hear

everything; even though a dead silence had set in, I could hear that silence. At that point there was some kind of convulsive movement – and suddenly, against my will, I opened my eyes.

She was looking straight into my face, and the revolver was now at my temple. Our eyes met, but remained there no more than a moment. I forced my eyes shut again, and in the same instant took a mighty resolve neither to open them nor to move one muscle, no matter what awaited me.

It really does happen sometimes that a person who is sound asleep suddenly opens his eyes, even raises his head for a second and looks around the room, and then, a moment later, puts his head back on the pillow and goes to sleep again, remembering nothing. When I, on encountering her gaze and feeling the revolver at my temple, suddenly closed my eyes again and lay motionless like one in a deep sleep – she might certainly have supposed that I was asleep and dead to the world, all the more so as it was quite improbable that I would have shut my eyes again at a moment *like that*, having seen what I had seen.

Yet, it was improbable. But even so she might still have guessed the truth – that was what had flashed through my mind so suddenly, all in a single instant. Oh, what a whirl of thoughts and sensations rushed through my mind in the space of less than a moment – and thank God for the electricity of human thought! If that were so (this was the feeling I had), if she had guessed the truth and knew I wasn't asleep, then by this time I might have vanquished her by my readiness to accept death, and her hand might easily be unsteady now. Her earlier determination might founder on this new, unprecedented discovery. It is said that people standing on high places have a kind of urge to throw themselves down into the abyss. I think that many suicides and murders owe their occurrence to the simple fact that the revolver was already to hand. That is also an abyss of a kind, a forty-five-degree slope down which it is impossible not to slide, and something irresistibly challenges you to pull the trigger. But her awareness that I had seen everything, knew everything and was waiting silently for death at her hands – that might hold her back on the gradient.

The silence continued, and I suddenly felt next to my hair, at my temple, the cold touch of iron. You may ask: did I really hope to survive? I will answer you, and this is God's own truth: I had no such hope, except that there was perhaps one chance in a hundred. Why was I lying there waiting for death? But I will ask in turn: what good was life to me after a revolver had been lifted against me by the being whom I worshipped? What was more, I knew with all the strength of my being that between us, at that very moment, a struggle was taking place, a terrible duel to the death, the duel that ought to have been fought long ago by that coward of yesterday who had been drummed out of the regiment by his friends for cowardice. I knew this, and she knew it too, if she'd guessed the truth – that I wasn't asleep.

Perhaps there was none of that, perhaps I didn't think that at the time, but all the same it must have been like that, even though I wasn't conscious of it, because I've done nothing but think about it every hour of my life ever since.

But again you will ask the question: why didn't I rescue her from her evil doing? Oh, I've asked myself that question a thousand times – each time that, with a chill running down my spine, I've remembered that second. But in those days my soul was in dark despair: I was going to my ruin, I myself was going to my ruin, so how could I rescue anyone? And how do you know that I wanted to rescue anyone at the time? How do you know what I might have been feeling?

My consciousness was seething, however; the seconds went by in dead silence; she was still standing over me – and suddenly I started with hope! I quickly opened my eyes. She was no longer in the room. I got out of bed: I had conquered – and she had been vanquished for ever!

I went through to the samovar. We always had the samovar set up in the main room, and it was always she who poured the tea. I sat down at the table without saying anything and accepted a glass of tea from her. Some five minutes later I took a glance at her. She was terribly pale, even paler than she had been yesterday, and she was looking at me. And suddenly – and suddenly, seeing that I was watching her, she gave me a pale smile with her pale lips, a timid question in her eyes. 'So she still has her doubts and she's wondering: does he know or doesn't he, did he see or didn't he?' I averted my gaze indifferently. After we had had tea I closed up the shop, went down to the market and bought an iron bedstead and a folding screen. Returning home, I instructed that the bed be placed in the main room and partitioned off by the screen. This bed was for her, but I said not a word to her about it. Even without words, that bed told her that I 'had seen everything and knew everything', and that the matter was no longer in any doubt. I left the revolver on the table overnight, as always. That night she climbed into the new bed without comment: the marriage was dissolved, she had been 'vanquished, but not forgiven'. That night she started to grow delirious, and by the morning she had developed a fever. She lay in bed for six weeks.

Chapter Two

A DREAM OF PRIDE

Lukerya has just told me that she won't stay on with me, and that as soon as the mistress has been buried she'll be leaving. I knelt down and prayed for five minutes; I wanted to pray for an hour, but I keep thinking and thinking and they're always morbid thoughts and my head aches – so where's the point in praying? It's just a sin! It's also so strange that I don't feel sleepy: when a person's in great sorrow, in really great sorrow, after the first violent outbursts he always feels sleepy. They say that men who have been condemned to death sleep very soundly on their last night. And that's how it should be, that's nature's way, otherwise their strength wouldn't last out . . . I lay down on the sofa, but I didn't go to sleep . . .

. . . All during the six weeks she was ill we looked after her day and night – I, Lukerya and a trained sicknurse from the hospital whom I'd hired. I didn't grudge the money, I positively wanted to spend money on her. I called out Dr Schroeder and paid him ten roubles a visit. When she came to herself again I began to make myself less conspicious. But why do I include that, anyway? When she was up and about again, she would sit quietly, without saying anything, at a special table which I'd also bought for her that time ... Yes, that's the truth, we were completely silent; or rather, we actually began to talk after a while, but it was all – just the usual things. Of course, I was purposely saying no more than was strictly necessary, but I could see very well that she too was relieved not to have to say anything she didn't absolutely have to. To me this seemed entirely natural on her part: 'She's taken a terrible battering and suffered a terrible defeat,' I thought, 'and she really ought to be allowed to forget about it and get used to things as they are.' So we stayed silent, but at every moment I was inwardly preparing myself for the future. I thought she was too, and I derived a huge amount of interest from wondering what it was she was thinking about now.

There's more, too: oh, no one could possibly ever know what I went through as I grieved over her in her illness. But I kept my grieving to myself, kept it shut up inside me so that not even Lukerya was aware of it. I could not imagine, could not even contemplate that she should die without knowing everything. When she was out of danger and her health had begun to return, I remember that I very quickly calmed down. Not only that: I decided to *put off our future* for as long a time as possible, and in the meanwhile leave things as they were. Yes, something strange and peculiar happened to me then, I can find no other words to describe it: I had triumphed, and that was enough to satisfy me completely. In that fashion I passed the entire winter. Oh, I was satisfied, as I had never been satisfied before, and for a whole winter at that.

There was in my life, you see, a certain terrible outward circumstance that until this time – until, that's to say, the catastrophe involving my wife – had weighed on me every hour of every day. This was the loss of my reputation and my departure from the regiment. To sum it up briefly: a tyrannical injustice had been done to me. It's true that my companions didn't like me because they found me difficult, ridiculous, even, though after all it's often the case that the things one considers exalted, intimately precious and revered are at the same time for some reason a source of amusement to the multitude of one's companions. Oh, I was never liked, not even at school. I have always been universally disliked. Not even Lukerya can bring herself to like me. That regimental incident, even though it was a consequence of the men's dislike of me, none the less bore an accidental character. I say this because there is nothing more hurtful and unendurable than to go to one's ruin because of an incident which might easily not have taken place, because of an unfortunate chain of circumstances that might have drifted by like passing clouds. For any being of intelligence, such a thing is degrading. The incident in question was as follows:

I was at the theatre, and at the interval I went out to the buffet. The hussar A—v suddenly came in and, in front of all the officers who were present, began telling two of his fellow-hussars in a loud voice that Bezumtsev, the captain of our regiment, had just created a scandal in the passageway and 'seemed to be drunk'. The conversation went no further, however, and there must have been some mistake, for Captain Bezumtsev wasn't drunk and the scandal was really no scandal at all. The hussars started to talk about something else and the matter ended there, but the following day the anecdote percolated to our regiment, and at once everyone started saying that I had been the only person from our regiment in the buffet, and that when the hussar A—v had said insolent things about Captain Bezumtsev, I had not gone up to A—v and stopped him by upbraiding him. But why should I have? If he had some personal axe to grind with Bezumtsev, that was their affair, and why should I interfere with it? But the officers, meanwhile, began to say that it wasn't a personal matter, that it affected the regiment, and that since I was the only one of our officers who had been there, I had shown to all the other officers and members of the public who had been in the buffet that there might be officers in our regiment who were not that fussy when it came to their own personal honour and that of the regiment. I was unable to agree with this analysis. They gave me to understand that I could still put things right if now, even at this late hour, I would have the matter out formally with A—v. I didn't want to do that, and as I felt irritated it was with some degree of arrogance that I refused. Immediately after that I sent in my papers – and that's the whole story. I resigned my commission proud but dispirited. My will and intellect had sunk to a low ebb. At about this time it came to pass that my sister's husband in Moscow dissipated our meagre fortune, including my part of it –

it was only a tiny part, but losing it put me out on the street without a copeck. I could have taken a civilian job, but I didn't: after wearing that glorious uniform I couldn't just go and work as a railway clerk somewhere. No – if it were to be shame, let it be shame, if it were to be disgrace, let it be disgrace, if it were to be degradation, let it be degradation, and the worse the better – that was what I chose. Then three years of gloomy memories, and even the Vyazemsky. A year and a half ago my godmother, a rich old lady, died in Moscow, unexpectedly leaving me, among various others, 3,000 in her will. I thought for a bit and then decided on my fate. I decided to open a pawnshop, asking pardon from no one: money, then a place to live – and a new life far away from my old memories – that was the plan. Even so, the gloomy past and my forever-ruined reputation tormented me every hour, every minute of my days. But then I married. By chance or not – I don't know. But in taking her into my household, I thought I was taking a friend; I was so badly in need of a friend. I had a clear perception, however, that the friend would have to be trained, given a finishing, conquered, even. And could I have explained anything straight away to this sixteen-year-old girl, with the sort of prejudices she had? For example, how could I, without the providential help of that strange catastrophe with the revolver, have persuaded her that I wasn't a coward and that in my regiment I'd been accused of being one unjustly? But the catastrophe had come at the right time. Having withstood the revolver, I had avenged the whole of my gloomy past. And although no one knew about it, *she* did, and to me that was everything, because she herself was everything to me, all the hope for my future that lived in my dreams! She was the only person I was going to make ready for myself, I had no need of anyone else – and now she had learnt everything – she had learnt, at least, that she had been unjust in hurrying to join the ranks of my enemies. This thought had delighted me. In her eyes I could no longer be a villain, but at the most only a strange person, yet even that thought after all that had taken place did not altogether displease me: being strange is not a sin – on the contrary, I intentionally postponed the denouement; what had taken place was still more than enough for my peace of mind and contained more than enough pictures, more than enough material for my dreamings. That was the bad thing – that I'm a dreamer: I had enough material, and what I thought about her was that *she could wait*.

In this manner the entire winter went by – in a kind of expectation of something. I used to like to watch her in stealth, as she sat at her little table. She used to do sewing of linen and underwear, and in the evenings she sometimes read books which she borrowed from my bookcase. The choice of books on those shelves must also have testified in my favour. She scarcely ever went anywhere. Each afternoon before dusk, after dinner, I used to accompany her on a walk, and we took our exercise, though not in total silence as before. Indeed, I tried to make it seem as though we had put all that behind us and were communicating amicably but, as I noted earlier, we were both trying to avoid saying any more than was strictly necessary. I was doing it on purpose; I thought it was essential to 'give her time'. It was, of course, strange that almost all winter it never occurred to me that there I was, fond of watching her in secret, yet never, all winter, had I caught so much as a glance from her! I thought it was timidity on her part. Then again, her illness had left her with a look of such timid meekness, such helplessness. No, it was better to wait, and – 'and she'll come to you of her own accord . . .'

This thought was a source of irresistible delight to

me. I should add one thing: sometimes I seemed to purposely work myself up and get my mind and spirit into a state where I actually began to nurse a grudge against her. And so it continued for some time. My hatred was never able to mature or take root in my soul, however. And even I myself felt as though it were only a kind of play-acting. Even though by buying that bed and screen I'd torn up our marriage, I was never, never able to see her as a criminal. And not because I took a lenient view of her crime. But because I intended to forgive her completely, right from the very first day, even before I bought the bed. Well, that was really a strange thing on my part, as I'm strict from a moral point of view. On the other hand to my eyes she seemed so defeated, so humiliated, so crushed, that I sometimes felt agonizingly sorry for her, even though for all that I sometimes found the idea of her humiliation an appealing one. The idea of that inequality between us was appealing . . .

That winter I purposely did several good deeds. I overlooked two debts and I gave one poor woman some money without demanding any pledge from her. And I didn't even tell my wife about this, I didn't do it with any hope that she might find out about it; but the woman herself came to thank me, almost on her knees. So word of the incident got round; it seemed to me that she was pleased when she heard of it.

But spring was coming, we were now halfway into April; we took out the double window-frames, and the sun began to brighten our silent rooms with brilliant pencils of light. But scales hung before my eyes and obscured my mind. Fateful, terrible scales! How did it come to pass that they fell away and I suddenly began to see clearly and understand everything? Was it an accident, or did some appointed day arrive when the sun's rays kindled a thought and a conjecture in my torpid mind? No, there was no thought, no conjecture – it was a nerve that suddenly started to play up, a nerve that had grown numb quivered, came to life and illuminated all my torpid soul and the devilish pride it contained. At the time, it was as if I'd suddenly leapt to my feet. It happened instantly and without warning, as evening was approaching, at about five o'clock, after dinner.

THE SCALES SUDDENLY FALL

A couple of words by way of preamble. A month ago I observed in her a strange pensiveness – not silence, really, but pensiveness. This was also something I noticed suddenly. She was sitting at her needlework at the time, her head bent down as she sewed, and she didn't see me looking at her. And suddenly it struck me how thin and drawn and pale she'd grown, her lips had lost their colour – this, together with her pensiveness, made an extreme and instant impression on me. I'd already heard her little, dry cough, especially at nights. I at once got up and set off in order to ask Dr Schroeder to call, without saying anything to her.

Dr Schroeder arrived the following afternoon. She was very surprised, and looked now at Schroeder, now at me.

'But there's nothing the matter with me,' she said with a vague, ironic smile.

Schroeder didn't examine her very thoroughly (these doctors are sometimes condescendingly offhand), and merely told me in the other room that it was the aftermath of her illness, and that when spring came it might not be a bad idea to take her to the seaside or, if that were impossible, simply rent a dacha in the country somewhere. In other words, he didn't say anything except that she was bit weak or something. When Schroeder had gone she suddenly said to me again, looking at me with the utmost seriousness:

'There's really nothing, nothing at all the matter with me.'

But, having said it, she suddenly reddened, evidently from shame. It was quite evidently shame. Oh, now I understand: she was ashamed that I was still *her husband*, that I was still concerned for her as though I were a real husband. At the time, however, I didn't understand this and ascribed her colouring to humility (the scales!).

And then, a month after this, at five o'clock on a bright, sunny April afternoon, I was in my shop doing my accounts. Suddenly I heard her, through in our bedroom, where she sat at her needlework, quietly, quietly . . . singing. This novel event really shook me, and to this day I haven't been able to fathom it out. Until that day I'd almost never heard her sing, except perhaps during the very first days after I brought her into my household, when we were still able to have some fun, doing shooting practice with the revolver. In those days her voice was still quite strong – resonant, though unsteady, but wonderfully sweet and wholesome. Now, however, her little song was faint as faint – oh, not mournful (it was some romance or other), but as though in her voice something had cracked, broken, as though it were not equal to the task, as though the song itself was ill. She was singing with only half a voice and, suddenly, as she got up, it broke off – such a poor little voice, and how pitifully it broke; she coughed to clear her throat and again, quietly, quietly, only just audibly, began to sing . . .

People will think my agitation ridiculous, but no one will ever be able to understand why I was so agitated! No, I didn't yet feel sorry for her, it was something quite different. Initially, for the first few minutes at least, I suddenly experienced a sense of bewilderment and terrible surprise, terrible and strange, morbid and almost vengeful: 'She's singing, and while I'm here, too! *Has she forgotten about me, or what?*'

Completely shaken, I remained where I was, then suddenly got up, took my hat and went out, almost without reflection. At least, I didn't know where I was going, or for what purpose. Lukerya began holding my coat out for me to put on.

'She's singing,' I found myself saying to Lukerya. She

didn't know what I meant, and looked at me, still at a loss for comprehension; and indeed I really must have been hard to fathom.

'Is this the first time she's sung?'

'No; she sometimes sings when you're not here,' Lukerya replied.

I remember everything. I descended the stairs, went out on to the street and set off wherever my legs would take me. When I reached the corner I began to look into space. People were going by, they pushed into me, but I didn't feel anything. I hailed a cab and told its driver I wanted to go to Politseysky Bridge. But then I suddenly abandoned the idea and gave him a twenty-copeck bit.

'That's for the inconvenience I've put you to,' I said, laughing inanely in his direction; but a kind of rapture had suddenly begun to affect my heart.

I went home, quickening my steps. Those poor, cracked, broken little notes had suddenly begun to jangle within my soul again. I caught my breath. The scales were falling, falling from my eyes! If she could sing in my presence, that meant she'd forgotten about me – that was what was so clearly and terrifyingly evident. That was what my heart felt. But the rapture was shining in my soul, and it overcame my terror.

Oh, irony of fate! I mean, there had been nothing in my soul all winter, could have been nothing in my soul all winter but that rapture, yet where had I been all the time? Had I been privy to my own soul? I ran up the staircase in a tremendous hurry, and I don't know whether my entrance was a timid one or not. All I remember is that the whole floor seemed to surge up like a torrent, down which I floated. I went into the room, she was sitting where she had been before, sewing with her head bent down, but she wasn't singing now. She gave me a fleeting and uncurious glance, but it wasn't really a glance at all, more a mere gesture, habitual and indifferent, the sort of glance one gives when someone comes into the room.

I went straight over to her and sat down on a chair right next to her, like a madman. She looked at me quickly, as though she were frightened: I took her arm, and I don't remember what I said to her, or rather, that is, what I wanted to say, because I couldn't even speak properly. My voice kept failing me, and I couldn't get it to obey me. And anyway, I didn't even know what to say, but just kept gasping.

'Let's talk ... you know ... why don't you say something?' I suddenly babbled, stupidly – oh, what did I care about being sensible?

Again she started and recoiled in a violent fright, looking at my face; but suddenly – a look of *stern surprise* appeared in her eyes. Yes, it was surprise, and at the same time *stern*. She was looking at me with those big eyes of hers. This sternness, this stern surprise dumbfounded me: 'So you're still after love, is that it – love!' was the question her surprise seemed to be asking, even though she said nothing. But I could read it all, all of it. A jolt passed through my whole being, and I simply tumbled in a heap at her feet. Yes, I fell at her feet. She quickly leapt up, but using extreme force, gripping her by both arms, I managed to detain her.

And I completely understood my despair, oh, I understood it all right! But, would you believe it, such uncontainable rapture was seething in my heart that I thought I was going to die. I kissed her feet in rapture and happiness. Yes, happiness, boundless and infinite, and this in spite of understanding the whole extent of my despair! I wept, tried to say something, but was unable to get the words out. Her fear and surprise were suddenly replaced by some anxious thought, some extreme question, and she looked at me strangely, wildly even, she was trying to grasp something quickly, and she smiled. My kissing her feet had embarrassed her terribly and she slid them away, but I at once proceeded to kiss the place on the foor where one of them had rested. She saw this and at once began to laugh with embarrassment (you know how it is when people laugh with embarrassment). She was beginning to be affected by hysteria. I could see that – her hands were fluttering. I didn't give that any thought, but began muttering to her that I loved her, that I wouldn't get up. 'Let me kiss your dress ... pray to you like this all my life.' I knew nothing, was conscious of nothing – and suddenly she began to sob and shake all over; a terrible fit of hysteria had set in. I had frightened her.

I carried her over to the bed. When the fit had passed, sitting up on the bed, with a look of terrible misery she seized my arm and asked me to calm myself: 'That's enough, don't torment yourself, calm down!' – and again she began to weep. All that evening I remained beside her. I kept telling her that I was going to take her to Boulogne, where they had the sea-baths, right now, or very soon, in two weeks' time, that her little voice sounded so cracked and dry, I'd heard it earlier that day; that I would close the pawnshop and sell it to Dobronravov, that we'd begin a new life, but the main thing was to get to Boulogne, Boulogne! She listened, but she was still scared. She was getting more and more scared. But for me that wasn't important, what mattered to me was my ever more intense and uncontainable urge to prostrate myself at her feet again, and again kiss, kiss the ground on which her feet had rested, and pray to her and – 'Beyond that I ask nothing, nothing more of you,' I kept repeating over and over again – 'Don't say anything, don't pay any attention to me at all, just let me watch you from the corner, turn me into your plaything, your lapdog . . .' She wept.

'*I thought you were just going to leave me like that*' – the words suddenly burst from her despite her will, so much despite her will that she was possibly quite unconscious of having uttered them, yet at the same time – oh, this was the most important, the most fateful thing she had ever said, something which that evening I totally understood and which seemed to slash my heart like a knife! It explained everything to me, everything, yet while she was beside me, before my eyes, I was filled with uncontainable hope and was terrifyingly happy. Oh, I had taxed her strength terribly that evening and I understood that, but I kept thinking that I could change everything in a flash! Finally, towards night-time, her energy completely gave out; I persuaded her to go to sleep, and she fell asleep at once, soundly. I had expected her to be delirious and she was, but only very slightly. I got up countless times during the night and went through quietly in my slippers to look at her. I wrung my hands over her, as I watched that sick creature on that wretched little cot, that iron bedstead I'd bought her that time for three roubles. I got down on my knees, but did not dare kiss her feet as she slept (without her permission!). I began to pray to God, but leapt back up again. Lukerya was watching me attentively, and kept coming out of the kitchen. I went in to her and told her to go to bed, saying that tomorrow everything would be 'quite different'.

And I believed that blindly, crazily, horribly. Oh, it was rapture, rapture that flooded my being! I longed only for the next day. And above all, I didn't believe there would be any disaster, in spite of the symptoms. My powers of reason had still not quite returned, even though the scales had fallen from my eyes, and it was a long, long time before they did – oh, not until today, this very day!! And how, how could it have returned then? I mean, then she was still alive, she was right here in front of me, and I in front of her: 'Tomorrow she'll wake up and I'll tell her everything, she'll see it

70

all.' That was the way I thought at the time: simply and clearly, hence my rapture! The main thing was that trip to Boulogne. For some reason I thought Boulogne was everything, that Boulogne was the very last word, the be-all and end-all. 'To Boulogne, to Boulogne! . . .' It was in a state of distraction that I waited for the next day to arrive.

III

I UNDERSTAND ONLY TOO WELL

I mean, this only happened a few days ago, five days, just five days ago, last Tuesday in fact! But, but . . . if only there'd been a little more time, if she could have waited a bit longer I'd – I'd have dispelled the murk! It wasn't as though she hadn't recovered her calm, after all. On the next day she listened to me with a smile, in spite of her confusion . . . The main thing was that during all that time, all those five days, she suffered either from confusion or from embarrassment. She was scared too, very scared. I don't argue that, I wouldn't be so foolish as to try to deny it: there was fear in her, but then, I mean, how could there not have been? After all, we'd long since become strangers to each other, grown detached from each other, and then suddenly all this . . . But I didn't pay any attention to her fear – new horizons were shining! . . . It's true, it's undoubtedly true that I made a mistake. Possibly even many mistakes. Even when we woke up that next morning (this was Wednesday), I immediately made a mistake: I suddenly turned her into my friend. I was in a hurry, far, far too much of a hurry, but I had to confess to her, and do more than confess! I told her straight out that I'd do nothing all winter but try to be certain of her love. I explained to her that the pawnshop had merely been a failure of my will and intellect, my own personal idea of self-torture and self-glorification. I told her that I really had been a coward that time in the theatre buffet because of my character, my lack of self-confidence; I'd been startled by the situation, by the people in the buffet and by the thought: 'How can I just suddenly fight a duel with him like that – surely it will seem stupid?' It wasn't the duel I was scared of; it was that the whole thing would appear stupid . . . and later on I didn't want to admit it and made everyone's life, including hers, a misery because of it, and then married her in order to make her life even more of a misery because of it. Most of the time I talked as though I were in fever. She herself took me by the hand and begged me to stop: 'You're exaggerating ... you're torturing yourself' – and again her tears would begin, again she would be close to hysterical seizure! She kept begging me not to say any of this, not to remember any of it.

I paid no attention to her pleas, or hardly any: all I could think of was spring, Boulogne! There was the sun, there was the sun of our new life, that was all I could talk of! I closed the shop and transferred the business to Dobronravov. I suddenly proposed to her that we should give away everything to the poor, with the exception of the fixed capital of 3,000 roubles that we had received from my godmother in her will, which we would use for a trip to Boulogne, and then come back and begin our new working life. And so it was decided, for she didn't say a word ... she just smiled. I think also that she smiled more out of tact than anything else, in order not to upset me. I mean, I could see she found me irksome, don't think I was so stupid or such an egoist that I couldn't see that. I saw it all, right down to the last detail, I saw it, I was more aware of it than anyone – the whole extent of my despair was on public view!

I told her about myself and about her, too. Even about Lukerya. I told her that I had wept ... Oh, I mean, I changed the subject, I too was doing my utmost not to mention certain things. And I mean, she even livened up a couple of times – I remember it, I remember it! Why do you say that I looked and saw nothing? Oh, if only *this* hadn't happened, everything would have come alive again. I mean, she told me only the day before yesterday, when the conversation turned to the subject of reading, and of the books she had been reading that winter – I mean, she began to tell me their plots, and she laughed when she remembered that scene between Gil Blas and the Archbishop of Grenada. And what childlike laughter it was, so sweet, just as it used to be before we were married (a moment! a moment!); how glad I was! Actually, that story about the Archbishop made a tremendous impression on me: I mean, she must have found so much peace of mind and happiness, in order to be able to laugh like that while reading that kind of a *chef-d'oeuvre* as she sat through the winter. She must already have begun to grow completely resigned, begun to believe completely that I was going to leave her *like that*. 'I thought you were going to leave me *like that*' – I mean, that was what she said on the

Tuesday! Oh, thought of a ten-year-old child! And I mean she believed, she really believed that everything was going to remain *like that*: she at her table and I at mine, and so both of us would live until the age of sixty. And suddenly – I come up to her, her husband, and the husband wants love! Oh, my lack of understanding, oh, my blindness!

I also made a mistake in looking at her with rapture the way I did; I should have exercised restraint; as it was, my rapture scared her. But I mean, I did exercise restraint, I stopped kissing her feet any more. Never once did I make a show of ... well, of being her husband – oh, that was never anything that was on my mind, all I did was pray! But I mean it was impossible for me just to keep silent, I couldn't just stop talking altogether! I suddenly told her that her conversation gave me pleasure and that I considered her incomparably, incomparably more educated and intelligent than myself. She blushed terribly, and said in an embarrassed kind of way that I was exaggerating. Then, out of foolishness, losing my self-control, I told her what rapture I'd experienced when, standing there behind the door, I'd overheard her duel, the duel of innocence and that brute, and what pleasure I'd derived from her intelligence, her brilliant wit and her childlike simplicity of manner. She sort of shuddered all over, began to babble something again about how I was exaggerating, but suddenly her whole face clouded over, she covered it with her hands and began to sob . . . At that point my endurance gave out: I again fell down before her, again began kissing her feet and the scene ended in another fit, just as it had on the Tuesday. This was yesterday evening, and the next morning . . .

The next morning? I must be out of my mind – why, the next morning was today, just a little earlier today!

Listen and try to grasp what I'm saying: I mean, when we met by the samovar this morning (this was after her fit of yesterday), I was actually shocked at how calm she was – that's what I'm trying to tell you! Yet all night I'd been quivering with terror about what happened yesterday. But suddenly she came up to me, put herself face-to-face in front of me and, folding her arms (this morning, this morning!), told me that she was a criminal, that she knew it, that her crime had been tormenting her all winter, and was tormenting her even now . . . that she deeply valued my generosity . . . 'I will be your faithful wife, I will respect you . . .' At that point I leapt to my feet and, like a madman, embraced her! I kissed her, kissed her face, her lips, like a husband seeing his wife for the first time after a long separation. The only thing is, why did I go out this morning, though it was only just for two hours ... to get our foreign passports ... Oh, God! If I could just have come back five minutes, five minutes earlier! ... And then that crowd at our front gate, those gazes trained on me ... Oh, Lord in Heaven!

Lukerya says (oh, I shan't let Lukerya go now, not for anything, she knows it all, she was here all winter, she'll tell me the whole story), she says that after I'd left the building, and only some twenty minutes before I came back – she suddenly went into our bedroom to ask the mistress something, I don't remember what, and she saw that she'd taken her icon out (that same icon of the Holy Virgin), that she had it in front of her on the table, and looked as though she'd just been praying before it. 'What's wrong, mistress?' 'Nothing, Lukerya, off you go, now ... Wait, Lukerya,' she said, went up to Lukerya and gave her a kiss. 'Are you happy, mistress?' 'Yes, Lukerya.' 'The master should have come and asked you to forgive him long ago, mistress ... Thank God you've made it up together.' 'Good, Lukerya, now go, Lukerya,' she said, and she smiled in that way of hers, and a strange way it was. So strange, that Lukerya suddenly came back ten minutes later in order to take a look at her: 'She was standing by the wall, right over by the window; she was resting one arm against the wall and leaning her head on that arm, standing there thinking. And so deep in thought was she that she wasn't aware of me watching her there from the other room. I could see she was sort of smiling, standing there, thinking and smiling. I looked at her, then turned round quietly and went out; but then I suddenly heard the window being opened. I immediately went in to say: "It's cold, mistress, watch you don't catch a chill," and suddenly I saw that she'd got up on to the window-sill and was standing there, at full height, in the open frame with her back turned against me and the icon in her hands. At once my heart sank, and I shouted: "Mistress, mistress!" She heard me, moved as though she were about to turn round to face me, but didn't, instead took a step forward, pressed the icon to her bosom and – threw herself out of the window!'

The only thing I remember is that when I went in through the gate she was still warm. That, and the fact that they were all looking at me. At first there was shouting, but then they all suddenly fell silent, and then all at once they parted in order to let me through and ... and she was lying there holding the icon. I have a dim memory of going up to her without saying anything and looking at her for a long time, and of everyone standing round me and telling me something. Lukerya was there, but I didn't see her. She says she spoke to me. The only person I remember is that tradesman: he kept shouting to me that 'a handful of blood came out of her mouth, a handful, a handful!' and directing my attention to the blood that was right there on the stone paving. I think I touched the blood with my finger, stained my finger, looked at it (I remember that), and he kept saying to me: 'A handful, a handful!'

'What do you mean, a handful!' I howled, they told me, with all might, raised my arms and threw myself at him ...

Oh, monstrous, monstrous! Misunderstanding! Improbable! Impossible!

IV

ONLY FIVE MINUTES TOO LATE

Don't you think so? Was it really something that might have been considered probable? Can one really say that it was possible? Why, for what did this woman die?

Oh, believe me, I understand; but the reason for her death is still a question, all the same. She was scared of my love, she asked herself seriously whether she should accept it or not, and preferred to die rather than endure the dilemma. I know, I know, there's no good cudgelling my brains over it: she made too many promises, she got scared she wouldn't be able to keep them – that's clear. There are some things about the situation that are completely awful.

Because why did she die? That's the question that won't go away. It keeps hammering, hammering at my btain. I would only have left her *like that* if she'd wanted things to remain *like that*. She didn't believe it, that's what it was! No – no, I'm talking nonsense, it wasn't that at all. It was simply because she had to do the honest thing where I was concerned; if she loved me she would have to love me entirely, and not in the way she'd have loved the merchant. And just as she was too chaste, too pure to consent to the kind of love the merchant wanted, so she didn't want to deceive me either. She didn't want to deceive me with half a love, or a quarter of one masquerading as a whole one. She was far too honest, that's what it was! And there was I trying to instil breadth of heart into her, remember? A strange notion.

I am horribly curious: did she respect me? I don't know – did she despise me or not? I don't think she did. It's horribly strange: why did it never once all winter occur to me that she despised me? I was utterly convinced that the opposite was true, right up until that moment when she looked at me with *stern surprise*. The *sternness* of it. I took it to mean at once, right there and then, that she despised me. It sank in irrevocably, for ever! Oh, I thought, let her despise me all her life if need be, but – let her live, let her live! Even this morning she was still walking, living! I totally fail to understand why she threw herself out of the window! And how could I even have imagined such a thing just five minutes earlier? I've called Lukerya. I won't let Lukerya go, not for anything, not for anything!

Oh, it was still possible that we might have reached some arrangement. It was just that we'd become such terrible strangers to each other during the winter, but was it really out of the question that we could have got used to each other again? Why, why couldn't we have become intimate again and begun a new life again? I'm generous, and so was she – there was our point of contact! Just a few more words, two more days, no more, and she'd have understood everything.

The thing that hurts most of all is that it was all a matter of chance – pure barbaric, inert chance! That's what hurts! I was five minutes, only five minutes too late! If I'd just arrived five minutes earlier – the moment would have drifted by like a cloud and would never have entered her head again. And the end of it would have been that she understood everything. But now it's back to empty rooms again, and once again I'm on my own. There's the pendulum ticking away, it's not interested, it's not sorry about anything. Now there's no one – that's the terrible thing!

I pace about, I keep pacing about. I know, I know, don't tell me: you think it's absurd for me to be complaining about chance and those five minutes, don't you? But I mean, it's obvious. Consider one thing: she didn't even leave a note behind her saying, 'Do not blame anyone for my death,' the way people usually do. Could it really not have occurred to her that she might cause trouble for Lukerya? 'You were alone with her,' they might have said, 'so you must have pushed her.' At any rate, had it not been for that fact that four people who had been looking out of the windows of the outbuilding and up from the yard at the time saw her standing in the window holding the icon and throw herself out, Lukerya would have been hauled in regardless. But, I mean, that was chance too – the fact that people were standing there and saw it happen. No, all that was a moment, just one unaccountable moment. A sudden, surprise attack, a burst of fantasy! So what if she was praying in front of the icon? That doesn't necessarily mean she was preparing for death. The whole moment lasted maybe some ten minutes in all, and the whole decision was made right at the time when she was standing against the wall, leaning her head on her arm and smiling. The idea flew into her head, made it spin, and – she couldn't keep her balance because of it.

Whatever you say, it was clear misunderstanding. She could still have gone on living with me. What if it was anaemia? What if it was simply caused by anaemia, by the exhaustion of her vital energies? She'd got tired during the winter, that's what it was . . .

I was too late!!!

How thin she is in her coffin, how pointed her little nose has grown! Her eyelashes are like arrows. And I mean, the way she fell – didn't crush anything, didn't break anything. Just that 'handful of blood'. A dessert-spoonful, in other words. Internal damage. A strange thought: what if I could just not bury her? Because, if they take her away, then . . . oh, no, it's almost unthink-able that they should take her away! Oh, I mean, I know they've got to take her away, I'm not a madman and I'm not raving, on the contrary, I've never been so lucid – but what am I to do like this with no one else in the place again, with just the two rooms and myself alone with the pawned objects again? Ravings, ravings, ravings! I tortured her to death – that's what!

What are your laws to me now? What good to me are your customs, your manners, your way of life, your state, your creed? Let your judges judge me, let them bring me to court, your public court, and I will say that I confess to nothing. The judge will shout: 'Be silent, army officer!' And I will shout back at him: 'What makes you think you have the power to make me obey? Why has a dismal inertia destroyed what was dearest to me? Why should I care about your laws now? I disassociate myself from them.' Oh, it's all the same to me!

Blind, she's blind! She's dead, she doesn't hear! You

don't know what a paradise I would have protected you with. That paradise was in my soul, and I'd have planted it around you! Well, so you wouldn't have loved me – so be it, what of it? Everything would have been *like that*, everything would have stayed *like that*. You would have just told me all about it as a friend – and then we'd have laughed and rejoiced, looking each other joyfully in the eyes. That's how we would have lived. And if you'd taken a fancy to someone else – well, so be it, so be it! You'd have gone off with him laughing, and I'd have watched from the other side of the street . . . Oh, anything, if only she'd open her eyes again just once! For one moment, just one moment! If she'd look at me, the way she did this morning when she stood in front of me and swore to me that she'd be a faithful wife! Oh, she'd take it all in in one glance!

Inertia . . . Oh, nature! People are alone upon earth – that's the terrible truth! 'Is there anyone alive upon the plain?' shouts the Russian epic hero. I too am shouting, but I am no epic hero, and no one replies. They say that the sun gives life to the universe. The sun will rise and, when it does, look at it – what is it but a corpse? Everything's dead, and everywhere there are corpses. Only people are alive, and around them is silence –

that's the earth! 'People, love one another' – who said that? Whose teaching is that? The pendulum's ticking heartlessly, repulsively. It's two o'clock in the morning. Her shoes are on the floor by her little bed, as if they were waiting for her ... No, seriously though: when they come to take her away tomorrow, what will I do?

PENGUIN 60s CLASSICS

APOLLONIUS OF RHODES · *Jason and the Argonauts*
ARISTOPHANES · *Lysistrata*
SAINT AUGUSTINE · *Confessions of a Sinner*
JANE AUSTEN · *The History of England*
HONORÉ DE BALZAC · *The Atheist's Mass*
BASHŌ · *Haiku*
GIOVANNI BOCCACCIO · *Ten Tales from the Decameron*
JAMES BOSWELL · *Meeting Dr Johnson*
CHARLOTTE BRONTË · *Mina Laury*
CAO XUEQIN · *The Dream of the Red Chamber*
THOMAS CARLYLE · *On Great Men*
BALDESAR CASTIGLIONE · *Etiquette for Renaissance Gentlemen*
CERVANTES · *The Jealous Extremaduran*
KATE CHOPIN · *The Kiss*
JOSEPH CONRAD · *The Secret Sharer*
DANTE · *The First Three Circles of Hell*
CHARLES DARWIN · *The Galapagos Islands*
THOMAS DE QUINCEY · *The Pleasures and Pains of Opium*
DANIEL DEFOE · *A Visitation of the Plague*
BERNAL DÍAZ · *The Betrayal of Montezuma*
FYODOR DOSTOYEVSKY · *The Gentle Spirit*
FREDERICK DOUGLASS · *The Education of Frederick Douglass*
GEORGE ELIOT · *The Lifted Veil*
GUSTAVE FLAUBERT · *A Simple Heart*
BENJAMIN FRANKLIN · *The Means and Manner of Obtaining Virtue*
EDWARD GIBBON · *Reflections on the Fall of Rome*
CHARLOTTE PERKINS GILMAN · *The Yellow Wallpaper*
GOETHE · *Letters from Italy*
HOMER · *The Rage of Achilles*
HOMER · *The Voyages of Odysseus*

PENGUIN 60s CLASSICS

HENRY JAMES · *The Lesson of the Master*
FRANZ KAFKA · *The Judgement*
THOMAS À KEMPIS · *Counsels on the Spiritual Life*
HEINRICH VON KLEIST · *The Marquise of O—*
LIVY · *Hannibal's Crossing of the Alps*
NICCOLÒ MACHIAVELLI · *The Art of War*
SIR THOMAS MALORY · *The Death of King Arthur*
GUY DE MAUPASSANT · *Boule de Suif*
FRIEDRICH NIETZSCHE · *Zarathustra's Discourses*
OVID · *Orpheus in the Underworld*
PLATO · *Phaedrus*
EDGAR ALLAN POE · *The Murders in the Rue Morgue*
ARTHUR RIMBAUD · *A Season in Hell*
JEAN-JACQUES ROUSSEAU · *Meditations of a Solitary Walker*
ROBERT LOUIS STEVENSON · *Dr Jekyll and Mr Hyde*
TACITUS · *Nero and the Burning of Rome*
HENRY DAVID THOREAU · *Civil Disobedience*
LEO TOLSTOY · *The Death of Ivan Ilyich*
IVAN TURGENEV · *Three Sketches from a Hunter's Album*
MARK TWAIN · *The Man That Corrupted Hadleyburg*
GIORGIO VASARI · *Lives of Three Renaissance Artists*
EDITH WHARTON · *Souls Belated*
WALT WHITMAN · *Song of Myself*
OSCAR WILDE · *The Portrait of Mr W. H.*

ANONYMOUS WORKS

Beowulf and Grendel   *Buddha's Teachings*
Gilgamesh and Enkidu   *Krishna's Dialogue on the Soul*
Tales of Cú Chulaind   *Two Viking Romances*